The Kindness Quilt

Nancy Elizabeth Wallace

Marshall Cavendish Children

A portion of the proceeds from the sale of *The Kindness Quilt* will be donated to **READ to GROW**/the Gini Fund. **READ to GROW** is a nonprofit literacy organization that provides *Books for Babies* at birth to promote parent-child bonding and *Books for Kids* as they grow. It is an organization of individuals passionate about its mission who believe in the power and magic of words, of bringing the shared joy of reading to children and their families, and of hope for our future. For more information visit: www.readtogrow.org

Warm and special thanks to everyone at **READ to GROW**:
to Sarah Kyrcz, Marcy Beatty, and Madison United;
to Leslie B., Doe, Lorraine, Judy, Mary-Kelly, Kay, Nancy A., Leslie C., and Marley;
Also to Margery, Anahid, Virginia, and Brian;
to Bobbi, Claudia, Cyd, Diane, Robin, and Sally;
to my Mom, Alexine, and my husband, Peter;
to Cathy Seibyl;

and to Siena, Nina, Jackson, and Spencer

Text and illustrations copyright © 2006 by Nancy Elizabeth Wallace
Marshall Cavendish Corporation, 99 White Plains Road, Tarrytown, NY 10591
www.marshallcavendish.us

Library of Congress Cataloging-in-Publication Data
Wallace, Nancy Elizabeth.
The kindness quilt / written and illustrated by Nancy Elizabeth Wallace.—1st ed.
p. cm.
Summary: Minna does a lot of thinking about her project to do something kind, make a picture about what she did,
and share it with her classmates, but finally comes up with an idea that spreads to the whole school.
ISBN-13: 978-0-7614-5313-0
ISBN-10: 0-7614-5313-X
[1. Kindness—Fiction. 2. Conduct of life—Fiction. 3. Schools—Fiction.] I. Title.
PZ7.W15875Kin 2006
[E]—dc22
2005027074

The text of this book is set in Berling.
The art was created by using origami and found paper, markers, pencils, colored pencils, and crayons.
Book design by Virginia Pope
Lion and the Mouse paintings by Kerri Wessel

Printed in China
First edition
1 3 5 6 4 2

In memory of
Virginia Fowler-Mariotti
"Gini"

One Friday at sharing circle, Minna helped Mrs. Bloom hold up a large green book.

"I *love* stories!" Minna said.

"I do too," said Mrs. Bloom. "I'm going to read an Aesop fable."

Mrs. Bloom began reading . . .

Read to Grow

Today's
Classroom
Helper

Minna

 # The Lion and the Mouse

Long ago a tiny mouse was scampering through the jungle. By and by he came upon a great lion snoozing in the tall grass. The mouse was feeling playful so he plucked a blade of grass . . . and tickled the lion's nose.

"GrrrooooOOAR!" roared the lion, grabbing the little mouse in his huge padded paw. "What is this, an afternoon snack?"

"PLEASE, PLEASE, PLEASE don't eat me," begged the mouse. "Someday I will do something nice to help you."

"HA! HA! HA!" laughed the lion. "YOU help ME?" But he let the mouse go and fell back to sleep.

A few weeks later the mouse was scurrying home when he heard a terrible roar. There was his friend trapped in a net. The little mouse gnawed on the ropes with his sharp teeth and set the mighty lion free.

The Big Book of Aesop's Fables

When the story ended, Minna sat down.

Then Mrs. Bloom asked, "What's the moral of this fable?"

"I know! I know!" said Minna. "It's about kindness. The lion let the mouse go, and later the mouse helped the lion. I think they both felt happy about being kind."

Tyrone said, "It shows you can be kind whether you're little or big."

Lindsey said, "We should try to
do something kind every day."

Dave said,
"I'm kind to Noodles."

"Yes!" said Mrs. Bloom. "Kindness is a good thing for all of us to practice, no matter how big or small we are. I know that you are all very kind. So, let's celebrate kindness with a do-and-draw-and-share *Kindness Project*."

That night Minna told Mom, Dad, and Pip, "Mrs. Bloom wants us to DO something kind, then make a picture about it and take the picture in to school to share. It's a kind of *Kindness Project*."

"That's a wonderful idea," said Mom.

"But," said Minna. "I'm not sure what to do."

"We can help you with ideas," said Dad.

Early Saturday morning, before Mom and Dad got up, Minna read to Pip.

"Reading me books is a good idea for your kindness picture, Minna," said Pip.

Minna nodded. "But," she said, "I'm still thinking."

Before lunch Minna went with Mom to *Community Clean-Up Day.*

"Picking up litter in the park is being kind to our Earth," said Mom. "That could be an idea for your kindness picture."

Minna nodded. "But," she said, "I'm still thinking."

Later in the afternoon, Minna and Dad
cooked creamy carrot soup for supper.
Minna took a big jar
to their neighbors.

After supper Minna got a pencil and paper.

"Kindness, kindness," she whispered to herself. "There are lots of kinds of kindness."

Dad brought Minna a snack. "YUM!" said Minna.

"Sharing the soup with Mr. and Mrs. Checker could be an idea for your kindness picture," said Dad.

Minna nodded. "But," she said, "I'm still thinking."

"You can use
my new markers,
Minna," said Pip.
"Thanks!"

Minna started writing and drawing.

Later Mom tiptoed in.
She brought Minna
scissors and more paper.
   Minna smiled. "Thanks,
Mom."
   Then Minna started
cutting.

On Sunday afternoon, Minna looked at what she had written and drawn and cut out.

Reading books

A is for 🍎

to your little brother

My family helping me

Kindness is

Suddenly Minna knew what she wanted to do. She found her glue stick and got to work.

On Monday Minna took her artwork to school. She listened as Carrie, Tyrone, Kyle, and Lindsey shared pictures of their acts of kindness.

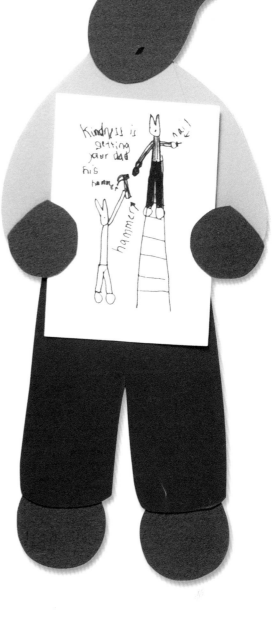

When it was Minna's turn, she held up her artwork.

"OOOOOO!" said the class.

"It looks like a beautiful quilt!" said Lindsey.

"WOW!" said Tyrone.

"If you want to, you can make yours look like a quilt too!" said Minna.

"Great!" said Mrs. Bloom. "Let's get out the art materials. Kyle, Carrie, Tyrone, Lindsey, since you shared your kindness art today, you can work on your quilt squares. Minna can help."

They cut and glued.

Then they taped their acts of kindness together.

Mrs. Bloom hung the paper quilt on the small bulletin board.

Kindness is

sharing your toys

Reading books to your little brother

sharing soap with your neighbors

Kindness is

picking up trash

trash here not here

My family helping me

Kindness is

setting the table without being asked

Kindness is getting your dad his hammer

nail

hammer

yay

yay

yay

yay

yay

cheer for the other team when your team wins

As the days passed, more acts of kindness happened.

Maya sent
a card.

Esteban helped his neighbor.

Amaan held a door open.

Dave took care of Noodles.

And the kindness quilt grew, until it overflowed the small bulletin board.

Mrs. Bloom and the children had to move it to the big bulletin board.

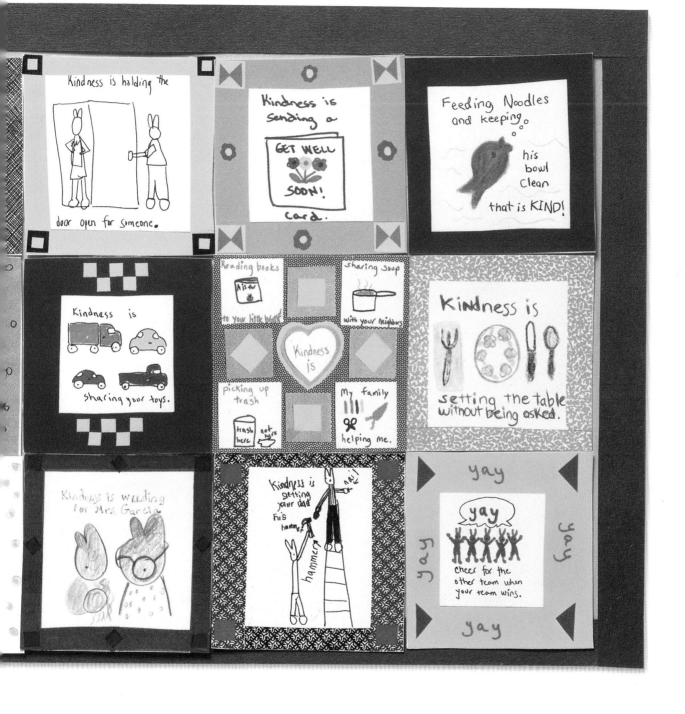

As more days passed, more and more acts of kindness happened.

Jadelyn was kind to Keisha.

Keisha was kind to Zack.

Zack was kind to A.J.

A.J. was kind to Minna.

When the kindness quilt overflowed the big bulletin board . . .

... Mr. Cooper helped them hang the quilt on the long wall in the hall.

Soon other classes joined in.

I RECYCLE CANS THAT'S BECAUSE I KIND TO OUR EARTH!

Kindness is

Taking out the trash.

sticking up for someone is Kind

I said "DON'T SAY THAT! That's MEAN!"

Kindness is keeping the bird feeder full in winter.

Kindness is asking your new neighbor to have a play date.

Sure!

I am teaching my little brother

how to swim.

Kindness is fixing your little sister's truck

And the kindness kept growing

and growing

Kindness is helping my mom water the plants

I help my little sister with her homework

$\frac{2}{+2}{4}$

HA HA HA HA

Telling your friend a joke is Kind

I helped my dad find his keys

helping Gran plant her garden

CARROTS

sitting next to your friend

when she is sad.

KINDNESS IS HELPING MY POP-POP TAKE OFF HIS SHOES...

kindness is teaching my little brother to spell

LOVE BIG BUG THE

Walking slow with your friend when he's got crutches is Kind

broken leg.

Kindness is feeding the baby her bottle

PLAYING WITH MY TWIN brothers IS KIND.

I cleaned the bath tub! My MOM said Thanks!

A lady bug was upside down. I turned it right side up so she could fly away. That was kind.

Kindness is lending a book to a friend.

Letting someone shorter stand in front of me at the parade

I made popcorn for my family.

Kindness is helping our Dad rake leaves

and growing!

Kindness is doing my chores without being asked.

When my little sister left her blankie in the grocery store I found it!

Bringing mrs. Z flowers

I made a card for Grandpa. Hi!

I helped the shed PAINT

I held the door for my friend

Help a turtle cross a road kind!

KINDNESS is helping my big sister make her bed.

Kindness is playing with the baby!

Sharing half a popsicle

Ms. Chodkowski's 5th grade